Contents

Riding Out After the Storm

When a great storm rolls into the South Australian Riverland, gusty winds whip up the Murray River. Twigs and leaves fly off tall gum trees, swirling in a jumble on the ground, and animals shelter cosily inside their homes. Sometimes big branches come crashing down, making new homes for ground animals. Old trees sometimes topple over to make way for young saplings.

One night, Jessie woke up to the sound of wind whistling around the house. Her bedroom window rattled and rain pounded onto the iron roof above her. Suddenly she felt a movement at the end of her bed and she sat up. Max the dog jumped into her arms and licked her face.

'Yuck, Max!' Jessie said. 'You can sleep on my bed but don't lick my face!'

Jessie slipped out of bed and drew back the curtain. Raindrops ran down the window and the dark branches of a gum tree waved in the distance.

Jessie climbed back into bed again and Max snuggled beside her. The storm raged outside but Jessie felt safe under her quilt. Mum and Dad always said that rain was like liquid gold. The more it rained the happier they were.

Jessie loved the rain too. It was just the wind she didn't like so much. She pulled the quilt over her ears so the rattling window wasn't so loud.

When Jessie woke up the next morning, the wind had stopped and all the rain had made the earth smell fresh. The trees and bushes were sparkling clean with the dust washed off their leaves. Even the air smelled brand new.

Jessie stretched, then dressed in her riding gear: long trousers, a long-sleeved shirt, hat and boots. This would be a great day for a ride on her pony, Magic.

'Hi, Jessie,' smiled Mum as Jessie hopped up on the kitchen stool to eat breakfast. A glass of orange juice and a big bowl of cereal were waiting for her. Mum was already working on the computer, sorting out business matters. Because she was looking forward to riding Magic, Jessie ate her breakfast very quickly. Then she hopped down and gave her Mum a big hug.

'Thanks for brekkie, Mum — I'm going to use up lots of energy riding my pony today!'

'Did you hear the storm in the night, Jessie?' asked Mum. 'There will be lots of branches down — maybe even whole trees, so be careful where you ride.'

Jessie finished the last of her juice and nodded.

'I'll be extra careful, Mum, promise.'

'Off you go then, and have fun.' Mum smiled at Jessie.

Jessie's eyes twinkled. 'We will!'

Dad was in the stables, brushing down his beautiful bay mare, Jezebel. Magic was nearby, snuffling about in a bag of oats.

'Hi, Dad,' greeted Jessie. 'Hello, Magic, my amazing pony!'

Magic had been a present for Jessie's seventh birthday. She remembered that day perfectly — it had been the most exciting day of her life! When she had pulled back the curtain in the lounge to look for Max, a beautiful buckskin pony had stared back at her through the window. It had been a dream come true.

Dad looked at Jessie. 'Well, Jess, I guess you're in a riding mood today, all dressed up in that riding gear!'

Jessie put her hands on her hips and gave her Dad a mischievous look.

'You got it, Dad! Would you please help me saddle up?'

'Sure. I've finished grooming Jezebel anyway. And it's about time Magic took his nose out of that empty bag of oats.'

Dad helped Jessie saddle up. Together they threw the saddle rug over Magic's back, then Dad lifted Jessie's leather saddle off the hook and buckled it neatly around the pony's girth. They stretched out Magic's front legs, checked his hoofs for stones, checked the stirrups and adjusted the reigns.

Jessie had become such a good rider that Dad sometimes gave her and Magic jobs to do around the farm. And after a storm, there were always lots of things to be done.

'So what do you think, Dad? Any jobs for us today?' asked Jessie.

Dad looked thoughtful for a minute. 'Tell you what, Jess. Why don't you and Magic check the fences?'

Jessie grinned. That was a good job. Sometimes a branch would land on a fence and crush it and the sheep would get out, or the cattle from next door would walk right in. Jessie's job was to report back to Dad where the fences were broken.

'Sure, Dad. Magic and I can do that, easy!' said Jessie.

'Great,' said Dad. 'Just check the fences in this paddock and the next one. I'll do the top paddocks later.'

Jessie and Magic set off happily. The fences were easy to follow, but it was important to walk alongside them carefully because after a storm there could be unexpected obstacles lying across the track.

'What a mess this storm has made, Magic!' exclaimed Jessie. Branches and twigs were lying everywhere. Jessie looked up into the high branches of the trees by the river.

'I wonder if the birds are all right. I bet some of them have lost their nests. They'll have to build new ones. And what about their poor little chicks?'

But all the birds seemed their usual selves. In fact, they were busier and noisier than ever. Pelicans glided across the river, a blue and white kingfisher sat on a low branch over the water waiting for a special fish for his lunch, and honeyeaters darted busily about the flowers, drinking the delicious nectar.

Jessie turned to ride along the next fence, when suddenly she spied something. There was a bird's nest lying on the ground — just in front of Magic's hoof!

'WHOA!' shouted Jessie as she shifted her weight back in the saddle. Magic

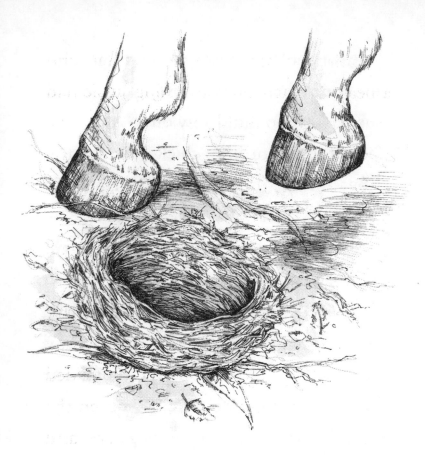

stopped immediately. Jessie leaned
forwards to look at the nest. There were
a few twigs and feathers scattered about,
but there was nothing in the nest. But
then, out of the corner of her eye, Jessie
saw a tiny movement beneath a twig.

At first, all she could see was fluff and a beak. It was the tiniest thing Jessie had ever seen. Looking more closely, she could just make out a head, eyes, little feet and a body that seemed to be half fluff and half skin.

Jessie was spellbound. Even Magic stood completely still.

Jessie knew straight away what she had to do. She carefully turned Magic away from the bird and the nest, and guided him towards a big old log resting on the ground. She stroked his neck and whispered in his ear. 'Now listen, Magic. You have to help me by not fidgeting. I'm going to slide off and I want you to keep still, okay?'

Jessie slipped her feet out of the stirrups and eased her right leg over

Magic's back. Then she slid easily to the ground, gathered the reins and tied them to the log.

She raised her finger to her lips and looked Magic in the eye, 'Shhhhh. Don't move, Magic.'

Jessie tiptoed over to the baby bird on the ground. She knelt down for a closer look. The bird looked up at her with its tiny brown eyes and made the faintest cheeping sound.

'Where are your mother and father?' Jessie asked softly. 'Don't they know where you are?' She looked up into the big trees and scanned the branches, but couldn't see any sign of its parents. 'Well you can't stay here,' she added. 'It's not safe. Do you want to come home with us?'

The baby bird fluttered its downy feathers as Jessie reached out to pick it up. But then Jessie paused. What could she carry it in? The only thing she could see was the broken nest. Then she had a great idea. She could carry the bird inside the nest, and tuck the nest inside her riding hat. Brilliant!

Jessie unfastened her hat and slipped it off her head. She scooped up the nest and packed it snugly inside the hat. 'Look, Magic. It's perfect!' she said. Magic snorted and flicked his long black tail.

Jessie carefully gathered up the baby bird and cupped it in her hands. She could feel its tiny, trembling body. Jessie knew she had found it just in time. She laid it gently in the nest and soothingly stroked its fluff.

'It's all right, you're safe now. You're coming home with us.'

Then Jessie realised that she couldn't ride Magic back to the house without wearing her riding hat. Mum and Dad had said she must never ride without her hat because it was too dangerous.

Jessie looked at the baby bird and shook her head. 'Guess what?' she sighed. 'We'll have to walk all the way home. And Magic, you'll just have to follow us.'

Jessie looped her arm through Magic's reins and set off home along the track. She carried the riding hat, with nest and baby bird inside, as carefully as she could. The tiny bundle of fluff didn't seem to be moving much anymore, but its beak opened now and then. Jessie hoped that Mum and Dad would know what to do.

They walked as quickly as Jessie could manage. Occasionally, Magic stopped to chew on a clump of grass, but then Jessie gave him a gentle tug on the reins to remind him that they were in the middle of a very important job — even more important than checking the fences!

It was a calm, cloudy day and the bush was quietly recovering from last night's storm. Even the leaves on the trees

and shrubs were still. Perhaps the bush was watching her, Jessie thought. Perhaps it was hoping that she could save the baby bird.

Jessie and Magic seemed to walk for ages along the sandy track by the fence. Jessie tried to hurry but her little legs were tired and her arms ached from carrying the riding hat steady for so long.

When they passed the big tree at the corner of the paddock, Jessie saw a cloud of dust. Then she heard the galloping hoofs of her father's horse, Jezebel, coming towards them.

'Dad!' called Jessie.

'Jessie!' he exclaimed, as he pulled up alongside her. 'What's wrong? Why are you walking?'

'Look,' said Jessie, holding up her hat to show him the baby bird in the nest.

Dad looked worried. 'Come on,' he said. 'Up behind me.' With his strong arms he reached down and pulled Jessie up behind him on the saddle. 'Don't worry about Magic,' he reassured her. 'He'll follow us home.'

Dad rode Jezebel back to the house. Jessie cradled the riding hat under one arm and held on tightly to her father's waist with the other arm. As soon as they arrived at the house he jumped off, grabbed Jessie and the hat, and they hurried inside.

Mum took one look at the tiny creature that was barely breathing and knew exactly what to do. Within a minute she had some special mixture in a small plastic dropper, like the ones doctors use, and was holding it to the fragile beak. Jessie held her breath, waiting to see what would happen. At first the bird didn't respond, but when a few drops went down its throat, the tiny creature started to cheep for more.

'Oh, look, it's alive!' said Jessie.

'And hungry too,' added Mum. She fed the tiny bird a few more drops of the precious mixture.

Dad carefully tucked the nest into a shoebox and Mum fitted a hot towel around the nest to keep it warm.

'Jessie,' said Dad, as he handed back her riding hat, 'you have done a very brave and wonderful thing. You have saved this little bird just in time.'

'Do you think it will be all right?' asked Jessie.

'I hope so, Jessie,' said Mum, making sure the baby bird was cosy. 'Thanks to you, I think it'll be just fine.'

Dad stood up and straightened his back. 'Right then, time to go and check the fences. The job's not finished yet. Coming with me, Jess?'

Jessie and Dad spent the rest of the morning riding beside each other, checking the fences. In a couple of places branches had fallen across the wire, so Dad and Jessie had to lift the branches off

and fix the fences. They rode all around the farm, but there was no major storm damage. Dad was relieved.

When they returned to the stables, Dad and Jessie were ready for a rest.

'Thanks, Dad,' said Jessie. 'That was fun. And Magic loved it too.'

'Good,' replied Dad. "I reckon Magic is getting used to this place, don't you?'

Jessie smiled. 'He loves it here. I know he does.'

'Well,' said Dad, 'I'd love a cup of tea and a piece of cake, but I guess we'd better clean up these horses first.'

'Sure,' agreed Jessie. 'And then we can see how my tiny baby bird is going.'

'Of course,' Dad nodded. 'I wonder if it's grown into an eagle yet?'

Jessie gasped. 'An eagle? Is that what it is?'

Dad laughed. 'No, I was joking. An eagle builds a great big nest and your bird has a small nest. I don't know what kind of bird it is.'

Jessie looked pleased. 'Then it will be a surprise when it grows up. And,' she added, 'I don't care what kind of bird it is, I know what its name is going to be.'

Jessie was very tired after cleaning the horses but as soon as she reached the front door of the house, she dashed inside to see her baby bird. She was delighted to find the tiny ball of fluff looking stronger and cheepier than ever.

'You are very special,' whispered Jessie into the nest, 'and I'm going to call you Storm.'

As she drifted off to sleep that night, Jessie knew the wild storm of the night before had brought her another adventure with Magic. It had also brought her another Storm that she'd never forget.

Magic Helps Out

One morning, Jessie woke up to the sounds of shouting and running. She jumped out of bed, ran to the front door and looked out into the yard. Jessie couldn't believe her eyes and squealed with delight at the funny scene in front of her. It reminded her of a circus she had seen where clowns squirted water all over each other.

Mum and Dad were running about with tools and hoses, calling here, racing there, and all the time a great fountain of water was spurting out of a broken pipe. Max was barking madly and running in and out of the spray, getting drenched and then shaking all over Mum and Dad who were already soaking wet.

Jessie could see that help was needed, so she ran outside at full speed. At once,

water sprayed her in the eyes and she couldn't see a thing, so she turned and ran away again. Then she had a brainwave.

Jessie raced into the shed and grabbed a big bucket. She dragged it back into the yard and placed it cleverly to collect some of the water squirting out of the pipe. She was soon dripping wet but she was very pleased with herself.

Dad was grappling with the break in the pipe when all at once the waterspout died away to a trickle. Dad stood up to stretch his back.

'What happened, Dad?' called Jessie, still giggling. 'Why did the water stop?'

'Mum turned off the pump, so we can fix this thing!'

'But my bucket isn't full yet,'

complained Jessie. 'It was going to be a special drink for Magic, so we didn't waste the water.'

At that moment Mum reappeared.

'Jessie, you look like a drowned rat!' she laughed.

Jessie grinned. She was standing in a mud pool in pyjamas and bare feet. There was water everywhere, and in the middle of it all was Dad. He was covered in mud and hacking at the broken pipe with a saw.

Jessie had another brainwave. 'Hey, Dad, I think we should build a proper fountain in the front yard. It could spray water all day.'

Mum took Jessie by the hand and led her towards the laundry. 'I don't think Dad's in the mood for fountain talk right now,' she said.

Jessie and Mum took off their dripping pyjamas in the laundry and rubbed themselves dry with towels.

'I've had enough,' laughed Mum, towelling her wet hair. 'And it's only eight in the morning! I hope the baby likes a bit of excitement so early in the day.'

Jessie wiped the mud from her face and looked at Mum in a puzzled way. 'What baby?' she asked.

Mum took Jessie's hands and placed them on her tummy.

'This baby,' replied Mum. 'Our baby.'

Jessie was silent for a moment. Then she burst out, 'Are we having a baby, Mum?'

'Sure are,' nodded Mum. 'You're going to be a big sister.'

'Wow,' said Jessie. 'Dad!' she squealed as her father appeared at the laundry door. 'I'm going to have a little brother or sister ... did you know that? I can teach it how to ride Magic and how to check the fences and feed the horses and round up the sheep and collect the eggs and bath Max and ...'

'Steady on,' laughed Dad. 'This baby's got a bit of growing to do before any of that can happen!'

Jessie broke into a big smile. The baby was great news, and she gave Mum and Dad a big hug. She didn't even mind that Dad was still dripping water all over her.

'Come on, time to get cleaned up,' said Mum. 'I'm starving.'

After a hot shower, Dad made them all breakfast.

'Around here,' he said, buttering the toast, 'babies have to get used to lots of excitement, don't they, Jess?'

Jessie nodded. 'Sure do! There's always something going on,' she agreed.

'Trouble is,' said Dad, 'now I'm way

behind on my day's work. I have to move the sheep into the top paddock today, but before that I have to run into town for some plumbing supplies so I can fix the pipe.'

Jessie looked hopeful. 'Can I help too Dad?'

He shook his head. 'Not really, Jess. I have to go all over the farm today. And some of the jobs I really need to do on my own.'

Jessie shrugged. But she had already made up her mind to do something useful. She just had to figure out exactly what that would be.

While Dad was in town, Jessie sorted out all the clothes in her drawers. She pulled out everything that was too small for her and filled a big bag to give to the baby. Nan had made her a beautiful party dress with pink and gold ribbons threaded through the stitching. Although it was her favourite dress, Jessie had grown out of it now. 'Hmm,' she said to herself, before slipping it into the bag. 'If I have a baby brother I don't know if he'll want to wear this very often!'

When the bag of clothes was full, Jessie sorted out toys and filled another bag. There were teddies and a toy car that she didn't play with anymore, and a few picture books.

But what could she do next? Mum was dozing in the bedroom and Jessie thought

it best not to bother her, especially with a baby inside her tummy that had some growing to do.

What Jessie really wanted was to ride her pony, Magic. All of a sudden she knew exactly what to do. She pulled on her riding gear and boots, grabbed her riding hat and tiptoed out the front door.

Magic was waiting for her in his stable. He snorted and flicked his black mane and tail. Jessie lifted the heavy saddle. Dad usually helped her get Magic ready but she knew how to do it. Luckily, Magic was very patient as Jessie buckled him up and stretched his legs. Jessie was sure Dad would be proud of her, saddling up all on her own, and she couldn't ask him for help anyway since he was so busy.

When everything was ready, Jessie led Magic to the fence rail. She climbed up and slipped easily into the saddle. It felt good to be on her pony again.

They walked and trotted around the paddock. Jessie could see the sheep in the next paddock standing around looking very bored.

'Poor sheep,' she said. 'They need something new to look at.'

And just then Jessie had yet another brilliant idea. It was a good day for great ideas, she thought. She could help Dad by moving the sheep for him! The sheep would be happy, her dad would be happy, and Jessie would have something really useful to do.

Jessie was excited. She hadn't moved the sheep by herself before, but she had helped heaps of times and it didn't seem too tricky. She made a plan.

Jessie rode Magic through the sheep paddock until she came to the gate. She would have to guide the sheep through this gate, then across the track and through the next gate into the top paddock. The sheep had done this a thousand times, so Jessie expected they'd know where to go.

First, Jessie had to open both gates. This meant she had to dismount from Magic, and then find a fence rail from which to mount him again. It was hard work already!

When the two gates were open, Jessie rode down around the sheep and began to round them up. Magic wasn't too keen on sheep and didn't want to get very close to them.

Jessie also had to teach him to turn sharply so they could stop the sheep moving in the wrong direction. Just when Jessie began to think it was all too difficult, the whole mob of sheep headed towards the first gate. She breathed a sigh of relief and took off after them. Magic thought it was fun now, and cantered back and forth happily, keeping the stragglers up with the mob.

At last the sheep crossed the track and reached the second gate, and through they went. Sheep always follow each other, and most of them wandered

through together into the top paddock. Jessie was feeling very pleased with herself.

There were only six sheep left in the bottom paddock now, and they were real slowcoaches. Jessie shouted at them to hurry up, and cantered up behind them. Suddenly they all took off through the gate. But the sheep in front turned down the track instead of going through the second gate and, of course, the other five sheep followed.

Jessie gasped. 'Silly sheep!' she yelled at them. 'Why did you do that? Can't you see where the others went?' Jessie groaned. 'What am I going to do now?'

The sheep inside the top paddock were grazing quietly on the grass already. Jessie slid out of the saddle and quickly shut the gate so they couldn't escape. Then she had to climb up onto the fence again to mount her pony. This was turning into really hard work, but Jessie couldn't give up now. She had a job to do!

The six runaway sheep had slowed down further along the track. Jessie walked Magic quietly along behind them, and tried to edge past them so they didn't scare. She hoped to be able to turn them around and head them back towards the gate. But one sheep decided to run and, of course, the others followed.

'Come back, silly sheep!' shouted Jessie.

The sheep kept running, with Jessie and Magic cantering behind, until they came to the open country. Now Jessie had a huge job to round these stragglers up and head them back up the track.

Jessie and Magic slowed to a walk again and Jessie looked around. She had never ridden Magic through this part of the farm. It was different. The trees were smaller and the ground was rockier. It wasn't as green here as down by the river. Jessie felt a little strange, as though she was in unfamiliar territory where she didn't belong.

The sheep were grazing quietly along the fence and Jessie walked Magic up behind. The sheep began to move back where she wanted them to go, but then at the last minute they turned away. Jessie slumped in her saddle. This was going to be impossible. What should she do?

She tried once more to guide the sheep back up the track, but again they refused to do what she wanted.

The sun was high overhead and Jessie was getting very hot. It was probably lunchtime, so she decided that the best thing to do was to get help. Jessie imagined Dad would be home from the shops by now and might even be upset with her, but she had to take the chance. It was better than staying out all day trying to round up six sheep and only driving them further and further away.

Magic was tired too, so Jessie sadly turned and guided him home.

When Jessie walked inside the house, hot and streaked with dirt, Mum and Dad didn't look too happy.

'Where have you been?' asked Mum. 'I've being looking all over the place for you.'

'And I was just coming to search for you,' growled Dad.

Jessie hung her head. 'I'm sorry,' she said. 'I've moved the sheep.'

Dad looked confused. 'You've done what?'

'I moved the sheep into the top paddock,' Jessie explained.

Mum scratched her head. 'On your own?'

Jessie nodded. 'Magic and I did it together,' she said.

'All the sheep?' asked Dad, still not believing his ears.

'Well, that's the problem,' admitted Jessie. 'All except for six.'

Dad found it hard to hide his grin. 'Hmmm,' he murmured. 'So where are the six?'

Jessie burst into tears. 'They escaped down the track!'

'Down the track, eh?' Dad said, nodding. 'Hmmm. That's happened to me before. Just a few silly stragglers, off down the track. Useless animals.'

Jessie looked up. 'That's what I think,' she sniffed.

'Right then,' said Dad. 'Let's have lunch. Then you and I will go and round up those stragglers. Did you shut the gates, Jess?'

'Yes,' nodded Jessie.

Mum gave Jessie a hug. 'Please don't disappear again, Jessie. I know you were trying to help, but next time tell us your plans first. Remember the rules?'

Jessie nodded and put her arms around Mum. All of a sudden she felt very tired.

'How's the baby?' she murmured, remembering the big news.

'Fine now,' said Mum. 'A little too much excitement for one baby in one day though. No more adventures today, please, Jessie!'

As they sat down to lunch, Jessie felt better. 'You know,' she said. 'I don't think Magic liked the sheep. But he still worked really hard.'

'So did you,' said Dad. 'We'll take it easy this afternoon. We'll go on the motorbike.'

Jessie grinned. Rounding up sheep on the motorbike with Dad sounded like another great adventure. She sneaked a glance at Mum, but Mum didn't seem to mind at all!

Animals in Magic's World

Cockatoo – type of parrot with a crest on its head

Echidna – a toothless burrowing mammal with spines like a hedgehog

Galah – a cockatoo with a rose-coloured chest and grey back

Honey-eater –a bird with a long tongue that can take nectar from flowers

Lizard – a reptile with a long body and tail and a scaly hide

Pelican – a waterfowl with a pouch in its beak for storing fish

Puggles – baby echidnas

Skink – a small lizard

A Pony Called Magic by Sheryn Dee